U0060709

For Dad

Speedy's Race

小快的比賽

Jill McDougall 著

王祖民 繪

"Let's have a race," said Kevin to Julie. "My turtle will race your turtle."

Kevin put his turtle, Jet, on the floor. Jet looked *fit and *keen.

*為生字，請參照生字表

Julie put her turtle, Speedy, on the floor next to Jet.

Speedy looked fat and *sleepy.

"This *string will be the *finish line," said Kevin. "Are you ready?" Julie looked at Speedy. His eyes were *shut. Was he *asleep? Julie had an idea. "Wait," she said as she ran off.

She came back with some *peas.

Speedy loved peas.

Julie put three peas on the finish line.

"Now we can race," she told Kevin.

5

Kevin had a toy gun.

"Get ready," he said. "Get set. Go!"

Bang! The gun went off.

Off ran Jet. He was fast. He ran past the TV. He ran past the chair. He ran *towards the finish line.

"Come on, Jet," cried Kevin.

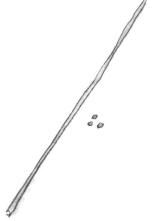

But where was Speedy? Julie looked around.

He had not moved.

"Come on, Speedy," she cried.

Speedy opened one brown eye. "Look," said Julie,

holding up the peas. "Yummy peas."

Speedy opened the other brown eye. And off he went.

Speedy ran fast.

He ran faster than Julie had ever seen him run.

But he was not running to the finish line.

He was running the other way!

Speedy ran past a *potted plant. He ran past another potted plant.

He ran all the way to *Nanna's feet. Then he stopped and looked at Nanna. She was eating *noodles.

Julie picked up Speedy and put
him on her hand.

"I win! I win!" cried Kevin.

Jet was on the finish line, eating peas.

"Okay," said Julie, "you win. But let's have another race tomorrow."

Julie had an idea.

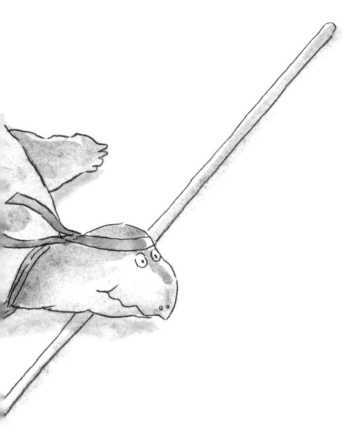

The next day, Kevin put his turtle, Jet, on the floor.

Jet looked keener than ever.

Julie put Speedy on the floor next to Jet.

Speedy looked more sleepy than ever.

"Are you ready for the race?" said Kevin.

"Not yet," said Julie. She had something in a bowl.

She put the bowl on the finish line.

"Now we can race," she told Kevin.

Kevin held up his toy gun.

"Get ready," he said. "Get set. Go!"

Bang! The gun went off.

Off ran Jet. He was *still very fast. He ran past the TV.

He ran past the chair. He ran towards the finish line.

"Come on, Jet," cried Kevin.

But where was Speedy?

Julie looked around.

He had not moved *again*.

"Come on, Speedy," she cried.

Speedy opened one brown eye.

"Look," said Julie, holding up the bowl.

"Yummy noodles."

Speedy opened the other brown eye.

And off he went.

Speedy ran fast. He ran faster than Julie had ever seen him run. But he was not running to the finish line. He was running the other way *again*!

Speedy ran past a potted plant. He ran past another potted plant. He ran all the way to Nanna's feet *again*. Then he stopped and looked at Nanna. She was eating fish soup.

Julie picked up Speedy and put him on her hand.

"I win! I win!" cried Kevin.

Jet was on the finish line, eating noodles.

"Okay," said Julie, "you win."

"Do you want another race tomorrow?" asked Kevin.

Julie looked at Jet. He was getting very fat from eating peas and noodles. Then she looked at Speedy. He was getting very fit from running fast.

"All right," said Julie. "We will have another race tomorrow."

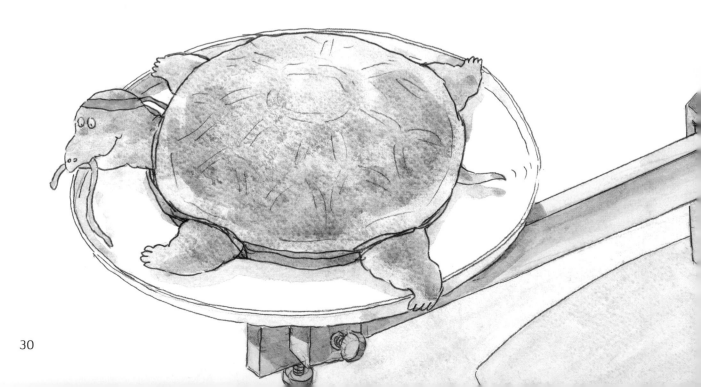

She picked up Jet and put him on her hand. "I *bet
you would like some yummy fish soup," she said.

生_{ㄕㄥ}字_{ㄗˋ}表_{ㄅㄧㄠˇ}

race [res] n. 比_{ㄅㄧˇ}賽_{ㄙㄞˋ} ；賽_{ㄙㄞˋ}跑_{ㄆㄠˇ}

p.2

fit [fɪt] adj. 健_{ㄐㄧㄢˋ}康_{ㄎㄤ}、強_{ㄑㄧㄤˊ}健的_{ㄐㄧㄢˋㄉㄜ˙}

keen [kin] adj. 積_{ㄐㄧ}極_{ㄐㄧˊ}的_{ㄉㄜ˙}

p.3

sleepy [`slipɪ] adj. 想_{ㄒㄧㄤˇ}睡_{ㄕㄨㄟˋ}覺_{ㄐㄧㄠˋ}的_{ㄉㄜ˙}樣_{ㄧㄤˋ}子_{ㄗˇ}

p.4

string [strɪŋ] n. 線_{ㄒㄧㄢˋ} ；細_{ㄒㄧˋ}繩_{ㄕㄥˊ}

finish line 終_{ㄓㄨㄥ}點_{ㄉㄧㄢˇ}線_{ㄒㄧㄢˋ}

shut [ʃʌt] adj. 閉_{ㄅㄧˋ}上_{ㄕㄤˋ}的_{ㄉㄜ˙}

asleep [ə`slip] adj. 睡_{ㄕㄨㄟˋ}著_{ㄓㄠˊ}的_{ㄉㄜ˙}

p.5

pea [pi] n. 豌_{ㄨㄢ}豆_{ㄉㄡˋ}

p.8

towards [tə`wɔrdz] adv. 朝_{ㄔㄠˊ}著_{ㄓㄜ˙} ……方_{ㄈㄤ}向_{ㄒㄧㄤˋ}前_{ㄑㄧㄢˊ}進_{ㄐㄧㄣˋ}

p.13

pot [pɑt] n. 花_{ㄏㄨㄚ}盆_{ㄆㄣˊ}

potted plant 盆_{ㄆㄣˊ}栽_{ㄗㄞ}植_{ㄓˊ}物_{ㄨˋ}

Nanna [`nænə] n. (口_{ㄎㄡˇ}語_{ㄩˇ}中_{ㄓㄨㄥ}的_{ㄉㄜ˙}) 奶_{ㄋㄞˇ}奶_{ㄋㄞ˙}

noodle [`nudl̩] n. 麵_{ㄇㄧㄢˋ}條_{ㄊㄧㄠˊ}

p.20

still [stɪl] adv. 仍_{ㄖㄥˊ}然_{ㄖㄢˊ}，還_{ㄏㄞˊ}是_{ㄕˋ}

p.32

bet [bɛt] v. 斷_{ㄉㄨㄢˋ}言_{ㄧㄢˊ}，確_{ㄑㄩㄝˋ}信_{ㄒㄧㄣˋ}

adj.=形_{ㄒㄧㄥˊ}容_{ㄖㄨㄥˊ}詞_{ㄘˊ}，adv.=副_{ㄈㄨˋ}詞_{ㄘˊ}，n.=名_{ㄇㄧㄥˊ}詞_{ㄘˊ}，v.=動_{ㄉㄨㄥˋ}詞_{ㄘˊ}

p.2

凱文對茱莉說：「我們來比賽，我的烏龜跟你的烏龜賽跑。」

凱文把他的烏龜——噴射機——放在地上。噴射機看起來又強健又積極。

p.3

茱莉把她的烏龜——小快——放在噴射機旁邊的地上。

小快看起來又肥又想睡。

p.4-5

凱文說：「這條線當終點線。你們準備好了嗎？」

茱莉看著小快，他的眼睛是閉著的。他是不是睡著了啊？

茱莉想到了一個點子，她一邊說：「等一下。」一邊跑走。

她帶了一些豌豆回來。小快愛吃豌豆。茱莉在終點線上放了三顆豌豆。

她對凱文說：「現在可以比了。」

p.6

凱文拿著一把玩具槍說：「各就各位，預備……開始！」

「砰！」一聲，槍聲響起。

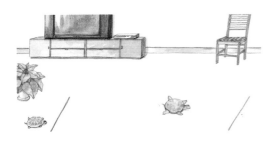

p.8

噴射機開始跑了起來。他跑得很快。他跑過電視機；他跑過椅子；他朝終點線跑過去了。

凱文大叫：「衝啊！噴射機！」

p.10

但是小快在哪裡呢？茉莉看了看四周，他根本沒動。茉莉大叫：「衝啊！小快！」

小快睜開一隻棕色眼睛。茉莉拿起豌豆說：「你看，好好吃的豌豆喔！」

小快睜開另一隻棕色眼睛。然後他跑了起來。

35

p.12-13

小快跑得很快。茱莉從來沒看過他跑得這麼快。可是他不是朝著終點線跑，而是往反方向跑過去！

小快跑過一個盆栽；他又跑過另一個盆栽；他一路往奶奶的腳下跑去，然後停下來看著奶奶。奶奶正在吃麵。

p.15

茱莉把小快拿起來放在手上。

凱文大喊：「我贏了！我贏了！」

噴射機已經到了終點線，正在吃著豌豆呢。

茱莉說：「好吧，你贏了。但是我們明天再比一次。」

茱莉想到了一個點子。

p.17

第二天，凱文把他的烏龜噴射機放在地上。噴射機看起來比以前更積極。

茱莉把小快放在噴射機旁邊的地上。

小快看起來比之前更想睡。

p.18

凱文說:「你們準備好要比賽了嗎?」

茱莉說:「還沒。」她在一個碗裡放了點東西,然後把碗放在終點線上。

她對凱文說:「現在可以比了。」

p.20

凱文舉起他的玩具槍說:「各就各位,預備……開始!」

「砰!」一聲,槍聲響起。

噴射機開始跑了起來。他還是跑得很快。他跑過電視機;他跑過椅子;他朝終點線跑過去了。

凱文大叫:「衝啊!噴射機!」

p.22

但是小快在哪裡呢?茱莉看了看四周,小快又不動了。她大叫:「衝啊!小快!」小快睜開一隻棕色眼睛。茱莉拿起碗說:「你看,好好吃的麵喔!」小快睜開另一隻棕色眼睛,然後他跑了起來。

p.25
小快跑得很快。茱莉從來沒看過他跑得這麼快。可是他不是朝著終點線跑，而是又往反方向跑過去了！

p.26
小快跑過一個盆栽；他又跑過另一個盆栽；他再次一路往奶奶的腳下跑去，然後停下來看著奶奶。奶奶正在喝魚湯。
茱莉把小快拿起來放在手上。

p.28
凱文大喊：「我贏了！我贏了！」
噴射機已經到了終點線，正在吃著麵條呢。
茱莉說：「好吧，你贏了。」
凱文問：「妳明天想要再比一次嗎？」

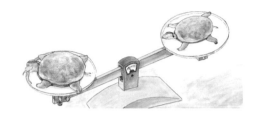

p.30

茱莉看著噴射機，他吃了豌豆和麵條之後，變得非常胖；然後她看看小快，他因為跑得很快，所以瘦了不少。

茱莉說：「好吧，我們明天再比一次。」

p.32

她把噴射機拿起來放到手上，說：「我敢說你一定會想來點好喝的魚湯吧。」

句型練習解答

② He looks angry.
You look bored.
Mom looks sad.
Debra looks tall.
The painting looks beautiful.
My uncle looks short and fat.

句型練習

Someone Looks....

在「小快的比賽」故事中，有很多關於 "Speedy looks...."（小快看起來 …… ）的用法，現在我們就一起來練習 "Someone looks...."（某人看起來 …… ）的句型吧！

① 請跟著 CD 的 Track 4，唸出形容「心情、外表等」的英文單字：

sad

fat

happy

bored

short

beautiful

tall

angry

② 請½仔™細™聽½ CD 的½ Track 5，利½用½左½頁½的½提½示™完½成½

以™下½的½句½子™：

Jet looks fit and keen.

Speedy looks fat and sleepy.

He looks _____.

You look _____.

Mom looks _____.

Debra looks _____.

The painting looks _____.

My uncle looks _____ and _____.

烏龜的移動方式

　　烏龜走路可是出了名的「慢吞吞」，因為牠們揹著重重的殼，既不能跑、也不能跳，只能慢慢的爬；即使遇到生命危險，牠們也沒有辦法加快速度逃跑，只能將頭、四肢跟尾巴縮進殼裡來保護自己，等到危險過去，再伸出來，繼續慢慢的、慢慢的往前爬。

　　不同種類的烏龜，腳的構造會有所差異，移動方式也不盡相同。例如以大海為家的海龜，腳通常會特別長，腳掌長得像槳一樣，讓牠在海裡能自在的撥動海水前進；可是一但到了岸上，失去海水的浮力，龜殼就會顯得特別笨重，這時候，海龜只好用不擅長走路的腳用力撥，拖著身體一點一點往前進了。

然而，習慣生活在陸地上的陸龜，雖然同樣也有笨重的外殼，但由於四肢上有堅硬的鱗片，可以減少爬行時摩擦的傷害，再加上腳上還有爪子可以抓住地面，同時支撐笨重的身體，因此陸龜能夠步行，而不會像海龜一樣，得辛辛苦苦的拖著身體前進。

　　除了海龜跟陸龜之外，還有一種烏龜叫做「澤龜」，主要生活在有水也有陸地的地方，故事中的小快跟噴射機就是屬於澤龜。為了適應週遭的環境，牠們的腳掌演化成既有蹼、也有爪子的構造，讓牠們不但可以在水中悠遊自在的游泳，也方便在陸地上行進。不過，牠們前進的方式還是跟其他烏龜一樣，總是一副慢吞吞的模樣。看牠們不疾不徐、一步一步前進的樣子，是不是覺得很有趣呢？

寫書的人

Jill McDougall is an Australian children's writer whose first book, "Anna the Goanna," was a Children's Book Council Notable Book. Jill has written and published over eighty titles for children including short stories, picture books and novels. Jill enjoys yoga, cooking and walking her two dogs along the beach.

畫畫的人

　　王祖民，江蘇蘇州市人。現任江蘇少年兒童出版社美術編輯副編審，從事兒童讀物插圖創作工作，作品曾多次在國際國內獲獎。作品《虎丘山》曾獲聯合國科教文野間兒童讀物插圖獎。

小烏龜大麻煩系列
Turtle Trouble Series

Jill McDougall　著／王祖民　繪

附中英雙語朗讀ＣＤ／適合具基礎英文閱讀能力者(國小4-6年級)閱讀

① 貪吃的烏龜小快 (Speedy the Greedy Turtle)　　④ 電視明星小快 (Speedy the TV Star)

② 小快的比賽 (Speedy's Race)　　⑤ 怎麼啦，小快？ (What's Wrong, Speedy?)

③ 小快上學去 (Speedy Goes to School)　　⑥ 小快在哪裡？ (Where Is Speedy?)

　　烏龜小快是小女孩茱莉養的寵物，他既懶散又貪吃，還因此鬧出不少笑話，讓茱莉一家人的生活充滿歡笑跟驚奇！想知道烏龜小快發生了什麼事嗎？快看《小烏龜大麻煩系列》故事，保證讓你笑聲不斷喔！

活潑可愛的插畫
還有突破傳統的編排方式
視覺效果令人耳目一新

幽默的文字，簡單的句型，
不會造成閱讀負擔

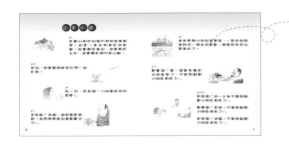

故事中譯保持英文原味，又可當成
完整的中文故事閱讀

書後附英文句型練習，加強讀者應
用句型能力，幫助讀者融會貫通

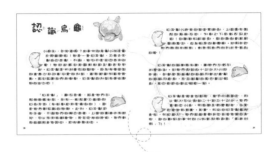

補充與故事有關的小常識，讓讀者
更了解故事內容

附英文生字表，幫助讀者了解故事內容

小老鼠貝貝歷險記系列
Tabitha and the Elephants

Marc Ponomareff 著／王平，倪靖，郜欣 繪／本局編輯部 譯

精裝／附中英雙語朗讀CD／全套六本

一隻機智勇敢的小老鼠，一隻真誠可愛的象寶寶，
六本為孩子量身打造的雙語繪本，
讓你在一連串驚險刺激的冒險故事中學英文！

① Tabitha Meets An Elephant　　　　　貝貝與小潔的相遇
② Tabitha and the Laughing Hyenas　　小老鼠貝貝與土狼
③ Tabitha and the Python　　　　　　小老鼠貝貝與大蟒蛇
④ Tabitha and the Crocodile　　　　　小老鼠貝貝與鱷魚
⑤ Tabitha Escapes from the Lions　　　小老鼠貝貝逃生記
⑥ A Party for Tabitha　　　　　　　　小老鼠貝貝的驚喜派對

國家圖書館出版品預行編目資料

Speedy's Race:小快的比賽 / Jill McDougall著;王祖
民繪;本局編輯部譯.－－初版一刷.－－臺北市：
三民，2005
　　面；　　公分.－－(Fun心讀雙語叢書.小烏龜，大
麻煩系列②)
中英對照
ISBN 957－14－4260－7　　(精裝)
　1.英國語言－讀本
523.38　　　　　　　　　　　　　　　94012413

網路書店位址　http://www.sanmin.com.tw

©　Speedy's Race
　　　──小快的比賽

著作人　Jill McDougall
繪　者　王祖民
譯　者　本局編輯部
發行人　劉振強
著作財　三民書局股份有限公司
產權人　臺北市復興北路386號
發行所　三民書局股份有限公司
　　　　地址／臺北市復興北路386號
　　　　電話／(02)25006600
　　　　郵撥／0009998-5
印刷所　三民書局股份有限公司
門市部　復北店／臺北市復興北路386號
　　　　重南店／臺北市重慶南路一段61號
初版一刷　2005年8月
編　號　S 805591
定　價　新臺幣壹佰捌拾元整
行政院新聞局登記證局版臺業字第○二○○號

有著作權　不准侵害

ISBN　957-14-4260-7　　(精裝)